The Giant Swing

Ready, Freddy!

Ready, Freddy!

The Giant Swing

by ABBY KLEIN

illustrated by
JOHN McKINLEY

Scholastic Inc.

To Gabe and Jonah,
two supercool kids!

No part of this publication may be reproduced, stored in a retrieval
system, or transmitted in any form or by any means, electronic,
mechanical, photocopying, recording, or otherwise, without written
permission of the publisher. For information regarding permission,
write to Scholastic Inc., Attention: Permissions Department,
557 Broadway, New York, NY 10012.

ISBN 978-0-545-55043-7

12 11 10 9 8 7 6 5 4 3 2   14 15 16 17 18 19/0

Printed in the U.S.A. 40

First printing, May 2014

CHAPTERS

I have a problem.
A really, really big problem.
The county fair is this weekend.
I love the fair, but I'm scared
of all the fast rides, especially
the Giant Swing.

Let me tell you about it.

CHAPTER 1

The Fair! The Fair!

"I can't wait for this weekend!" said Jessie as she took a bite of her turkey sandwich.

"I know. Me, neither," said Chloe, waving her pink fingernails in my face.

"Watch out," Robbie whispered to me. "She's flapping around like a pink flamingo, and she almost poked you in the eye."

I scooted closer to Robbie.

"It's my dance show, and I get to wear my brand-new pink ballet shoes and my brand-new pink tutu. They match my nails perfectly. See?" she said, waving her nails around again. "Did you know that the name of this nail polish is Ballet Pink?"

"No one cares, Little Miss Dancypants," said Max. "They're not talking about your dance show."

"They're not?" said Chloe, looking confused.

"No, I was talking about the county fair," said Jessie.

"The fair?" said Chloe. "Who cares about the silly old fair?"

"We do!" we all said together.

"I love looking at all the animals," said Robbie. "The cows, and the horses, and the sheep."

"I love the pigs," said Max.

"Ewwwwww. Peeeeuuuuwww," said Chloe holding her nose. "I hate pigs."

"Why don't you like pigs?" said Robbie. "Isn't pink your favorite color? I thought you were in love with anything pink."

"I do love pink," said Chloe.

"Really?" I whispered to Robbie. "We would have never guessed."

"But pigs are smelly, and muddy, and disgusting," said Chloe.

"Maybe to you," said Robbie.

"Yeah, maybe to you," said Jessie. "I think they are really cute."

"Kittens, like my little Fifi, are cute," said Chloe. "Not pigs."

"My favorite thing at the fair is the Watermelon Seed Spitting Contest," said Jessie. "I want to enter this year. My *abuela*, my grandma, has been teaching me how to spit the seeds really far. She used to do it all the time when she was a little girl in Mexico."

"Really?" said Max, talking with a mouthful of sandwich. A little piece of chewed-up bologna came flying out of his mouth and landed on Chloe's arm.

"Ewwww! Gross! Gross!" said Chloe, shaking her arm in the air, trying to get the food off.

"Watch out, Freddy," said Robbie. "The bird is flapping her wings again."

"No wonder you like pigs so much, Max. You are one!" Chloe shouted.

"What did you say?" said Max.

"You are a P-I-G, pig!" she yelled.

"Uh-oh," I said to Robbie. "Did Chloe just call Max a pig?"

Robbie nodded his head. We sat there frozen, wondering what Max, the biggest bully in the whole first grade, was going to do next.

All of a sudden Max started snorting like a pig in Chloe's face. "Oink, oink, oink! Oink, oink, oink!"

"Stop that! Stop that right now, Max," Chloe whined.

"Oink, oink, oink! Oink, oink, oink!" Max continued.

"I said stop!"

"But you said I was a pig, and this is what pigs do," said Max, snorting in her face.

"That's it! I'm moving and taking my lunch somewhere else," said Chloe. "I'm not going to sit here with a pig."

She packed up her ballerina lunch box and moved farther down the table.

"Good," said Max. "Now we don't have to listen to her anymore." He turned to Jessie. "So

OINK
OINK

what is your grandma's secret for spitting seeds really far?"

"I can't tell you," said Jessie. "It's a family secret. But I think I can win the contest this year."

"My favorite thing at the fair is the rides," said Max.

"I love the rides, too," said Robbie.

"Me, too," said Jessie. "The faster the better, right, Freddy?"

"Uh, right," I said.

"What are you talking about?" Robbie whispered to me. "You are afraid of the fast rides."

"I know," I whispered back. "But *they* don't have to know that."

"Which one is your favorite, Freddy?" asked Jessie.

"Umm . . . um . . . ," I stammered. I couldn't think of one. All of the rides I liked were not

scary. I wish I were as brave as Jessie. She isn't afraid of anything.

"He can't think of one," said Max, "because he's afraid of them all."

"That's not true," said Jessie. "Freddy is not a baby. He goes on all the rides. He just can't think of his favorite."

"Well, my favorite is the Giant Swing," said Max. "I bet you don't go on that one, do you, Freddy?"

"Of course he does," said Jessie. "Who would be afraid of swings?"

"Yeah," I said, trying to fake a smile. "Who would be afraid of swings?"

"But these aren't like the swings on the playground," said Max. "They are really big, and they spin around really fast. Sometimes I feel like I'm going to go flying out of the seat." Max laughed.

I gulped. That was exactly why I don't ever go on the Giant Swing.

"Well, you can see for yourself that Freddy isn't afraid to go on the swings," said Jessie. "We can all go on them together at the fair."

Great, I thought to myself. *Just great. Why did Jessie have to say that?*

Jessie put her arm around me. "Freddy is really brave. You'll see."

"Not as brave as you," I mumbled.

"We'll see how brave the little wimp is," said Max, snickering. "I bet he won't even get on."

"Oh really?" said Jessie. "What do you want to bet?"

"How about the winner gets the playground ball for a week at recess?" said Max.

"Deal," said Jessie.

Max laughed. "I can't wait to have that ball all to myself for a whole week."

"Dream on," said Jessie. "We're going to win the bet, and you're going to be super bored at recess without that ball. Right, Freddy?"

"Right," I mumbled.

Maybe I could get the flu by Saturday, and no one would know what a wimp I really was.

CHAPTER 2

Swinging Practice

That afternoon I sat next to Robbie on the bus ride home. "What am I going to do?" I moaned.

Robbie shook his head. "I don't know," he said. "This is a problem."

"Tell me about it," I said. "I think I'm going to throw up."

"Why didn't you just tell them you're afraid of the Giant Swing?" asked Robbie.

"Are you crazy? You want me to tell the

meanest, toughest kid in the whole first grade that I'm afraid to go on some ride at the fair?"

"But you are," said Robbie.

"But if I tell *him* that, then he's going to tease me and call me a baby, and I'll never hear the end of it!"

"So what are you going to do?" said Robbie.

"That's exactly what I asked you. You should be able to think of something. You're the genius!" I leaned my head back against the bus

seat and closed my eyes. "How did I get myself into this mess?"

Just then the bus pulled up to Jessie's stop. "What mess?" she said as she walked by my seat.

"What? Oh, nothing, nothing," I said.

"Well, see you at the fair," she said.

"Yeah. See you at the fair."

"I can't wait to see Max's face when you ride that Giant Swing," Jessie called as she ran off the bus. "He's going to wish he never made that bet."

"I wish *you* had never made that bet," I mumbled.

Robbie poked me in the arm.

"Ow, what did you do that for?" I asked.

"I have an idea," said Robbie.

"You do?" I said. "Are you going to mix up a magic potion with your chemistry kit and make me invisible?"

"No," said Robbie, laughing.

"Well, then, what is your great idea?"

"We can practice in your backyard," said Robbie.

"Practice what?"

"Swinging."

"But I already know how to swing," I said.

"I know," said Robbie, "but you're afraid of the Giant Swing because it spins in circles. We can practice that in your backyard."

"How?" I asked.

"I'll show you," said Robbie. "This is your stop. Come on!"

We jumped off the bus and ran into my house.

"Hi, boys," said my mom. "How was your day today?"

I looked at Robbie, and he looked at me. "Fine," we said together.

"Would you two like a snack?"

"No thanks, Mom," I said as I opened the back door. "We're going outside to play."

"Okay," said my mom. "Are you sure you don't want to take any snacks outside with you?"

"Yeah. We're sure," I called over my shoulder. I pushed Robbie out the door.

"We don't have any time to waste," I said. "The fair is tomorrow. So what is your great idea?"

"Freddy, you sit in the swing," said Robbie, "and then I'll twist the chain around and around."

"Then what?" I said.

"Then I'll let go," said Robbie, "and as the chain unwinds, the swing will spin around. It will be just like riding the Giant Swing."

"But I'll go flying off," I said.

"No, you won't," said Robbie. "Kimberly and I do this all the time at our house. It's actually really fun! You just have to hang on."

"Well, okay. I'll try it," I said.

"Great," said Robbie.

I stood there in the middle of the grass, not moving.

"Get your butt down on that swing. It doesn't work if you stand here in the grass."

I slowly walked over to the swing and sat down.

Robbie started to twist the chain of the swing around and around. "Ready, Freddy?" he asked.

"I guess so," I said.

"Okay," said Robbie. "I'll count to three, and then I'll let go. Just make sure you hold on. One . . . two . . . three!"

Robbie let go, and the swing started spinning around and around.

Without thinking, I let go of the swing to cover my eyes, and at that moment, I went flying off the swing and landed face first in the grass and dirt with a giant *THUD!*

"OOMPH!"

Robbie came running over. "Freddy! Freddy, are you all right?"

I picked up my head and spit some grass out of my mouth. *Pfft. Pfft.* Then I slowly sat up.

"I think so," I said.

"Why did you let go?" asked Robbie. "I told you not to let go."

"I know. I know," I said. "But I was really scared, so I had to cover my eyes."

"How about you just close your eyes if you're scared," said Robbie, laughing. "That way you can still hold on to the swing."

"Good idea," I said.

"Are you ready to try again?" asked Robbie as he helped pull me up out of the grass.

"As ready as I'll ever be," I said, brushing the dirt off my shirt. I walked back over to the swing and sat down.

"Now remember," said Robbie, "whatever you do, do not let go of the swing."

"Yes, sir," I said, giving Robbie a salute. "I will keep my hands on the swing."

Robbie twisted the chain around again. "Okay, here we go. One . . . two . . . three!" Robbie let go, and the swing started spinning again.

This time I did not let go. I squeezed my eyes shut and held on tightly to the swing. It seemed like it was spinning forever, and then it stopped.

Then I heard Robbie yelling, "You did it! You did it! You didn't let go!"

I opened my eyes slowly and looked around. I was still on the swing. "I did it! I did it!" I said.

I jumped off the swing and gave Robbie a big hug. "You are a genius," I said.

"Now you'll be able to go on the Giant Swing tomorrow with no problem," said Robbie. "And Max won't think you're a baby."

"Boy, I hope you're right," I said. "I hope you're right."

CHAPTER 3

Fraidy-Cat

That night at dinner my sister, Suzie, and I could not stop talking about the fair.

"I can't wait for tomorrow," said Suzie, wiggling in her seat.

"Me, neither!" I said, bouncing around in my chair.

"I can tell," said my mom. "The two of you can't sit still."

"What are you most excited about?" asked my dad.

"I don't know," said Suzie. "There are so many things. I don't know where to start!"

"Oh, me! Me! Me! Me!" I called out, waving my hand in the air.

"Hey, watch out!" said Suzie. "You almost got your fork full of mashed potatoes stuck in my hair."

My dad laughed. "This isn't school, Freddy. You don't need to raise your hand to talk."

"I can't wait to hold the baby chicks at the petting zoo," I said.

"Ooooo, they are so cute and fluffy," said Suzie. "Can I bring one home this year?"

"*You* bring one home? What do you mean *you*?" I said. "I asked first."

"No, you didn't," Suzie said.

"Yes, I did."

"No, you didn't."

"Yes, I did."

"All right. Enough, you two," said my dad.

"No one is bringing home any baby chicks," said my mom.

"How about just one, and we'll share it?" said Suzie.

My mom shook her head.

"Why not?" Suzie whined. "Freddy and I will take care of it. Right, Freddy? You won't have to do a thing, Mom."

"We'll do everything. I promise," I said.

My mom shook her head again. "The answer is no. You can hold them and cuddle with them at the fair, but you are not bringing a chicken into this house." She is such a neat freak. We're not allowed to have any pets in the house.

"I saw in the newspaper that there are going to be some new shows this year," said my dad.

"Really? Like what?" asked Suzie.

"Well, let's see . . . there is going to be a Monster Truck Show."

"No way!" I said, jumping up out of my chair. "I love Monster Trucks."

"What's a Monster Truck?" said Suzie.

"It's a big huge truck," I said, stretching my arms out wide.

"That's it?" said Suzie. "What's so great about a big huge truck?"

"Oh, they are awesome," I said. "They drive over stuff and crush it just like this," I said, smushing my fist into my mashed potatoes.

"Freddy!" my mom yelled. "Do not play with your food. Look at your hand. It's covered in mashed potatoes. Go wash it off in the sink."

I lifted up my hand and licked the potatoes off my knuckles.

"Ewwww, gross," said Suzie.

"Tomorrow I think I'm going to put you in the pen with the pigs," said my mom. "Now go wash up."

I washed my hands and sat back down.

"I'll tell you what I really can't wait for," said Suzie. "The rides!"

"Woohoo! The rides," I said, pumping my fist in the air.

"I'm not talking about the baby rides," said Suzie. "I'm talking about the big rides."

"I am, too," I said.

"Since when do you go on the big, fast rides?" said Suzie.

"I am this year," I said, trying to sound confident.

"Oh really?" said Suzie. "We'll see what happens when we get there. I think you're going to wimp out as usual."

"Suzie," said my mom, "be nice to your brother. Remember, he is a year older, so maybe the rides won't seem so big."

"Yeah," I said. "I'm older."

"But still a fraidy-cat," said Suzie.

"Suzie, if you don't have anything nice to say, then please keep your mouth shut," said my dad.

"Well, if you're so brave, then tell me what ride you are going to go on first?" Suzie asked me.

"The Giant Swing," I said.

"The Giant Swing? Ha!" said Suzie. "That thing whips around at like one hundred miles an hour."

My stomach did a flip. *Did she have to say that?* I thought to myself. Robbie didn't tell me that it went around that fast!

"I think I'm going to go upstairs now," I said, pushing my plate away. "I'm not hungry anymore." I actually thought I was going to throw up.

"What's wrong?" asked Suzie. "Feeling sick just thinking about the rides? What did I tell you? You're too much of a fraidy-cat to go on those big rides."

I stuck my tongue out at her and walked out of the room.

"Hey, Mom, Dad, did you see what he just did?" Suzie whined.

"He's just upset because you were teasing him," said my mom.

"Leave him alone," said my dad.

"Ugh!" groaned Suzie, and she followed me upstairs to my room.

"Go away!" I yelled. "Leave me alone!"

As usual, Suzie did not leave me alone. She walked right up to me and stuck her face in mine. "What is your problem, Stinkyhead? Too afraid to go on that ride alone?"

Hey, I thought to myself, *Suzie just gave me a great idea.*

"Yes, I am."

"You are?" Suzie said, sounding surprised.

"Yes, I am too scared to go on it alone. Will you go with me?" I would just tell Max that Suzie was the one who was too afraid to go on the ride alone, so I promised her that she could ride with me. That way I could have Suzie next to me on the ride, but Max would think that Suzie was the baby, not me.

"But I promised Kimberly that I would go on it with her," said Suzie.

"Just this one ride," I begged.

"What's it worth to you?"

"Ummm . . . how about some of the banana taffy I bring home from the fair?" I suggested.

"Not some. *All* of it," said Suzie.

"All of it? But you know that's my favorite treat from the fair."

"Take it or leave it." Suzie stuck her pinkie out for a pinkie swear. That's how we sealed all our deals.

"Fine, pinkie swear," I said as we locked our pinkies together.

I sighed. I guess no banana taffy was better than Max calling me a fraidy-cat for the rest of first grade.

CHAPTER 4

Ribbit, Ribbit, Ribbit

The next day my family went to the fair with Robbie's family.

"Let's go get our hair braided," said Suzie.

"Great idea!" said Kimberly. "I've always wanted to do that!"

"Well, I don't want to do that," said Robbie.

"I don't want to, either," I said.

"Why not?" Suzie said, laughing. "You two would look so cute with ribbons and beads in your hair."

"Ha, ha, ha! That's a good one, Suzie. I'm laughing just thinking about it," said Kimberly.

"Very funny," I said.

"Yeah. It's so funny I forgot to laugh," said Robbie.

"I have an idea," said Robbie's mom. "We'll take the girls to get their hair done, and you two can go with Freddy's mom and dad to do something you want to do. Then we'll meet at the petting zoo in a little bit."

"Good idea, Mom," said Robbie. "Freddy, what do you want to do?"

"I don't know. What do you want to do?"

"How about the Frog Jumping Contest?" said Robbie.

"Yes! Yes!" I said, hopping around. "The Frog Jumping Contest. Let's go to the Frog Jumping Contest!"

"The way you're hopping around, *you* could enter the contest," said my dad.

"Ribbit, ribbit, ribbit," I croaked as I hopped around some more.

"You're crazy," said Suzie. She grabbed Kimberly's hand. "Come on, Kimberly, let's get out of here."

The girls left to get their hair braided, and Robbie and I went to pick out frogs for the Frog Jumping Contest.

"Step right up. Step right up," said the man. "Pick a frog. Any frog."

Robbie and I walked over to the big tank full of frogs. "Which one are you going to pick?" I asked Robbie.

"I'm not sure," said Robbie. "First, I have to look at them carefully." Robbie stuck his nose against the glass wall of the tank and stared at the frogs. He was a science genius. He probably had some special way of figuring out which one could jump the fastest and the farthest. Finally, he pointed to a big fat green striped one and said, "I'll take that one."

The man reached into the tank, grabbed the frog, handed it to Robbie, and said, "Here you go. Hold on tight. Don't let it out of your hands until I say, 'Go!'"

"And how about you, young man?" he
said to me.

"I'll take that one with the dark brown
spots," I said.

"Okeydokey," said the man, and he handed
me the frog. It felt slippery and cool and wet
between my fingers.

I walked over to where my parents were
standing. "Isn't he cute?" I said.

"Ribbit, ribbit, ribbit," it croaked.

I lifted him up near my mom's face. "Mom, I think he wants to give you a kiss."

"AAAAAHHHHHHH!" my mom screamed. "Get that slimy thing away from me, Freddy."

I laughed. "It's just a frog, Mom. What are you so afraid of?"

"You're afraid of rides. I'm afraid of frogs," said my mom.

I was having so much fun with my frog that I had forgotten about the rides. Did she have to remind me?

I walked back over to Robbie. "What's your frog's name?" I asked him.

"Phib," said Robbie.

"Phib?" I said. "What kind of name is that?"

"It's short for 'amphibian.'"

"Am-phib-a-what?" I said.

"Amphibian," said Robbie. "Frogs are amphibians, which means they live both in the water and on land."

I shook my head. "Is there anything you don't know?" I said, laughing.

"How about you? What did you name your frog?" Robbie asked me.

"Larry," I answered.

Robbie burst out laughing. "Larry! How did you come up with that?"

"I don't know," I said, smiling. "I just kind of like it."

"The Frog Jumping Contest is about to begin," shouted the man. "Everyone, bring your frogs to the starting line."

As we were walking over to the starting line, I reached into my pocket to rub my lucky shark's tooth for good luck. Then I whispered to Larry, "You can do it, buddy. Show them what you got."

"Ribbit, ribbit, ribbit," said Larry.

Once all of the kids were at the starting line, the man said, "On your mark, get set, go!"

We all put our frogs down in the dirt and let them go.

"Go, Larry! Go, Larry!" I shouted.

"Go, Phib! Go, Phib!" Robbie yelled.

Everyone's frogs were jumping all over the place.

"You can do it, Larry!" I called out. "Keep jumping. Keep jumping!"

"Faster, Phib, faster!" Robbie screamed.

All of a sudden, Larry turned to the left and jumped right out of the track.

"Wait, Larry! Come back! Come back!" I screamed. "The race is over here. You're going the wrong way!"

I ran after him, but every time I was about to grab him, he hopped away.

"Oh no!" I cried. "Oh no!"

Larry was headed straight toward my mom. "Grab him, Mom!" I yelled. "Grab him!"

My mom just stood there, frozen.

"He's getting away. Grab him!"

All of a sudden, my mom bent down and caught Larry before he could hop away again.

I ran over to her. Larry was squirming around in her hands.

"Are you okay, Mom?" I asked. "You don't

look so good. Your face is the same color green as the frog."

"Quick!" said my mom, shoving Larry in my face. "Take this slimy thing away from me!"

I took Larry out of her hands and laughed.

"What's so funny?" she said.

"You held a frog!"

My mom laughed. "Yes, I guess I did," she said, smiling.

"I never thought I would see you do that!" I said.

"I never thought I would do it," said my mom. "Well, I guess there is a first time for everything."

"I guess there is," I mumbled.

If my mom could hold a frog, then I could go on the Giant Swing. Right? My stomach did a flip.

"Freddy, are you okay?" asked my mom. "Now *you* are the color of that frog."

I swallowed hard. "Yeah. I'm fine."

"Let's put the frog away and go find the girls," said my mom. "I've had enough of these green slimy things for one day."

"Did you hear that, Larry? She thinks you are slimy. I think you're cute," I said.

"Ribbit, ribbit, ribbit," Larry answered.

CHAPTER 5

The Petting Zoo

We left the Frog Jumping Contest and went to meet Suzie and Kimberly at the petting zoo.

"Look what I got!" Robbie said, holding up a blue ribbon. "My frog hopped across the finish line in first place!"

"Cool," said Kimberly.

"How about you, Freddy?" said Suzie.

"Ha, ha, ha," Robbie laughed.

"What's so funny?" asked Kimberly.

"Freddy's frog took a little detour," said Robbie.

"What do you mean?" said Suzie.

"He jumped out of the track and hopped right over to Mom," I said.

"To Mom?" said Suzie. "But Mom hates frogs."

"I know," I said. "But for some reason he really liked her! I think he wanted to kiss her!"

We all laughed.

"Let's go in the petting zoo," said Kimberly. "I can't wait to pet those baby chicks. Come on!"

"Mom, do you want to come in with me?" I asked.

"No, Freddy," my mom said, smiling. "I've had enough animals for one day. I'll just wait for you here."

All the kids went into the petting zoo. It was one of the biggest ones I had ever seen. There were goats, chicks, roosters, pigs, sheep, a llama, a camel, a calf, and two ponies.

"Wow! Look at that!" said Robbie. "A camel."

"That is so cool," I said. "I've never seen one this close before."

"Me, neither," said Robbie.

"Let's go pet it," I said.

Robbie grabbed my shirt. "Not so fast," he said.

"Why not?"

"Because I've read that camels aren't so nice," said Robbie.

"What do you mean?" I said.

"If they are angry or upset, they will spit."

"Ewwww!" I said, sticking out my tongue. "That's gross."

"I know," said Robbie. "I don't think I really want to get spit on by a camel. That has got to be super slimy and disgusting!"

"If he's so good at spitting, maybe we can train him to spit watermelon seeds, and he can beat Jessie in the Seed Spitting Contest," I said.

"That would be pretty funny," said Robbie.

"Look at that rooster," I said. "He looks like he has a white Mohawk on his head."

We walked over to it.

"Hey, dude, nice haircut," Robbie said to the rooster. "Freddy, maybe you should get your hair cut like that."

"Then I would look like a rock star," I said, pretending to play air guitar. "I could have my own band."

"And I could be in your band," said Robbie, pretending to play the drums.

Suzie and Kimberly walked up. "What are you two weirdos doing?" Suzie asked.

"Being rock stars," we said.

Kimberly shook her head. "Whatever," she said. "Come on, Suzie. Let's go find some more animals to pet."

"I want to hold one of those baby pigs," I said to Robbie.

"Me, too!" he said.

We went over to the piglets, and a lady asked, "Do you want to hold one in your lap and brush it?"

"Sure!" I said.

I sat down on the ground. The lady put a fat pink piglet in my lap and handed me a brush. "Here you go. Brush gently."

I started to brush the piglet and he snorted happily. *Oink, oink, oink.*

"I think he likes it," I said to Robbie.

Oink, oink, oink.

"I never knew that pigs had hair," I said.

"Of course they have hair," said Robbie. "They are mammals."

"So?"

"All mammals have hair or fur."

"You are like a walking encyclopedia of science," I said.

"I just love science," said Robbie.

"I wish I could have a pet pig," I said. "It could sleep with me on my bed every night and be my snuggle buddy."

"Good luck with that," said Robbie. "Your mom won't even let you have a cat or a dog. She would freak out if you ever brought a pig into the house!"

"But whenever I spilled food on the floor, she wouldn't have to get the vacuum out. My piggy could just eat up the mess!"

"Keep dreaming," said Robbie, shaking his head. "Keep dreaming."

We put the pigs down and went over to the lambs.

"These lambs are so soft and fluffy," I said.

"I wonder if this is what clouds feel like," said Robbie. "Wouldn't it be cool if you could touch the clouds?"

"Maybe some day you'll invent a jet pack for flying," I said, "and then humans will be able to fly up into the sky and touch the clouds."

"That would be so cool," said Robbie.

"So cool," I said.

"I'll be right back," said Robbie. "I'm going to get some of that food, so we can feed the animals."

"Okay," I said. "I'll wait here and pet this fluffball a little longer."

"Be back in a minute," said Robbie.

The lamb was so soft — even softer than my blanket at home. I bent down and rubbed my cheek against its head. Just then, I felt something tugging at the back of my shirt. "Hey, Robbie, cut it out!" I said.

I felt the tugging again. "Stop it!"

Then I felt it again. "It's not funny anymore. Leave me . . ." As I turned around to smack Robbie's hand away, I realized that it wasn't Robbie grabbing my shirt. And it wasn't Suzie. And it wasn't Kimberly. It was a goat!

"Hey! What are you doing?" I shouted.

The goat had my shirt in its mouth and was chewing on it.

"Hey! Stop it! Stop chewing my shirt!"

Robbie came back with the pet food. "What's going on?"

"This goat is chewing my shirt!" I yelled.

"Ha, ha, ha," laughed Robbie.

"It's not funny," I said. "This is one of my favorite shark shirts! Give him some food, so he leaves me alone!"

"Here, little goat," said Robbie, holding some pellets in his hand. "Come try some of this yummy food. I think it will taste better than Freddy's shirt."

The goat let go of my shirt and went to nibble the food in Robbie's hand.

I looked at the back of my shirt. "Oh no! Look! He chewed a hole right through my shirt!"

"All this talk of chewing is making me hungry," said Robbie. "Let's go get something to eat."

"Yeah. Let's get out of here before he chews my underwear!" I said.

CHAPTER 6

Cotton Candy, Caramel Apples, and Churros

"Freddy! What happened to your shirt?" my mom asked when we walked out of the petting zoo.

"You see that brown-and-white-spotted goat over there?" I said, pointing.

"Yes," said my mom.

"Well, I guess he didn't get enough breakfast this morning, so he needed a little snack, and he decided to eat my shirt!"

"That's hilarious!" Suzie said, laughing.

"No, it's not," I said, frowning.

"Yes, it is!"

"No, it's not! This is one of my favorite shark shirts!"

"Ha, ha, ha!" Suzie continued laughing.

"Stop it! Stop laughing!" I yelled.

"All right. Enough," said my dad. "Suzie, leave Freddy alone."

"Why don't we all go get something to eat?" suggested my mom.

"Great idea, Mrs. Thresher," said Robbie. "I'm starving, and I don't want to eat Freddy's shirt!"

We all walked over to the food area.

"I want a hamburger!" said Robbie.

"I want a hot dog," said Suzie.

"I want a chili dog," said Kimberly.

"What do you want, Freddy?" asked my mom.

"I want cotton candy, a caramel apple, taffy, and a snow cone, and . . ."

"That's for dessert," said my mom. "What do you want for lunch?"

"Cotton candy."

"Cotton candy is not lunch. You need to eat something else first," said my dad.

"Fine," I said. "I'll have a hamburger like Robbie."

The kids went to sit down while the parents got the food.

"I think we should go on the rides after lunch," said Kimberly.

The rides! I almost forgot all about the Giant Swing and Jessie and Max's bet. My stomach felt sick again.

"I don't think we should go on the rides right after lunch," I said.

"Why not?" said Suzie. "Are you being a fraidy-cat again?"

"No, I'm not being a fraidy-cat. I just don't want to throw up my hamburger all over you!" I said. "Remember, you are going on the Giant Swing with me. I don't think you want me barfing in your lap, do you?"

"No, I don't," said Suzie. "You're right. We'd better wait a little bit after we eat before we go on the rides."

"Okay, here we go," said my dad, as he put the food down on the table. "Two hamburgers, one hot dog, and one chili dog. Enjoy!"

"Hey, Dad. Did you get any of those little ketchup packets?" I asked.

"Yes, I did," he said. "They are right here in my pocket."

He pulled about six ketchup packets out of his pocket. "Here you go, Freddy. I think this should be enough. Do you need help opening them?"

"Nope. Thanks, Dad. I can do it myself."

My dad went to sit down with my mom and Robbie's parents.

I grabbed a ketchup packet. "I love, love, love ketchup!" I said.

"Really?" said Kimberly. "Do you love it so much that you are going to marry it?"

Suzie and Kimberly burst out laughing. "Ha, ha, ha, ha, ha!"

"No, I'm not going to marry it," I said, struggling to tear open the packet. "I'm going to put it on my hamburger."

The packet was really hard to open. I was twisting it and trying to bite it with my teeth. All of sudden, without warning, the top ripped off and squirted ketchup all over my face and my shirt.

Robbie, Kimberly, and Suzie thought it was so funny that they almost fell out of their chairs.

"Look! It's the ketchup monster!" said Robbie.

"You'd better be careful, or he might eat you up," said Suzie.

"Great! Just great!" I muttered to myself. "First the goat chews a hole in my shirt, and now I spill ketchup all over it."

I grabbed some napkins and wiped off my face and my shirt. Then I sat and ate my hamburger in silence.

My mom came over to the table. "Why are you so quiet, Freddy?"

"Nothing," I mumbled.

"I know how to cheer you up. How about some dessert?" she said.

I smiled.

"I knew that would make you smile," said my mom. "What would you like?"

"Cotton candy, a caramel apple, taffy, and a snow cone."

"You'll be sick if you eat all of that," my mom said. "Choose one."

"But it's so hard to choose," I whined. "I can't choose just one!"

"I want a cherry-flavored snow cone," said Kimberly.

"I want cotton candy," said Robbie.

"I want a caramel apple," said Suzie.

"Freddy, how about you? Have you decided yet?" said my mom.

"No. They're all so good. I still can't decide," I said.

"Don't take all day," said Suzie. "Make a decision."

I hit my forehead with the palm of my hand. "Think, think, think."

As I was thinking, someone came up from behind me and grabbed my shirt. I reached around and smacked a hand.

"Hey, what did you do that for, Freddy?" said Jessie.

"Oh, Jessie, it's you," I said. "Sorry about that. I thought you were a goat."

"A goat? What are you talking about?" said Jessie.

"This morning a goat chewed a hole in his shirt while we were in the petting zoo," said Robbie.

"Really?" said Jessie.

"Yep." I nodded. "So when I felt something pulling on the back of my shirt, I thought it was the goat!"

"No goat. Just me," said Jessie. "What are you guys doing?"

"Waiting for Freddy to decide what he wants to get for dessert," said Robbie.

"Why don't you have one of these?" said Jessie, holding up the treat she had in her hand. "It's delicious!"

"What is it?" I said.

"It's a churro."

"A what?"

"A churro. It's from Mexico. My *abuela* knows

how to make really good ones. It's a stick of
fried dough that's rolled in cinnamon sugar."

"I've never had it before, but it sounds
yummy," I said. "I think I'll have that!"

"You're going to love it," said Jessie. "You can
get them right at that booth over there. Why
don't you get one, and then meet me at the
Watermelon Seed Spitting Contest? It's going
to start really soon."

"Okay," I said. "See you there!"

CHAPTER 7

Spitting Seeds

Robbie got his cotton candy. I got my churro, and then we walked over to the Watermelon Seed Spitting Contest.

"Hi, guys," said Jessie. "Do you like that churro, Freddy?"

"It's delicious!" I said. "I can't believe I never tried it before. I just never knew what it was."

"I love trying new foods," said Jessie. "My *abuela* always says that you'll never know if you like something unless you try it."

"It tastes kind of like a doughnut," I said, licking some cinnamon sugar off my lips.

"You'd better eat that last bite because the Seed Spitting Contest is about to start," said Jessie.

I popped the last bite in my mouth and was quickly chewing it up when someone poked me in the back and yelled, "BOO!"

I jumped about three feet in the air, and chewed-up bits of churro came flying out of my mouth and landed on my shoe.

"Well, look who's here," said a voice. "If that's as far as you can spit, you'll never win this contest."

I didn't even have to turn around to know who it was. I would know that voice anywhere. I even hear it in my dreams . . . actually, my nightmares.

"Great," I mumbled to myself. "Just great."

"I've been looking for you guys all day," said Max.

"We haven't been looking for you," I whispered to Robbie.

"Are you ready, Freddy, to go on the Giant Swing, or is the little baby too scared?"

My stomach did a flip.

"Of course he's going to go on the Swing," said Jessie, "but right now it's time for the Seed Spitting Contest. Are you doing it, Max, or are you too afraid you're going to lose to a girl?"

"Ha!" said Max. "Very funny. Everyone knows that boys are better than girls at everything."

"They are not," said Jessie. "Girls can do anything boys can do."

"Yeah, right," said Max. "I'm going to win this contest for sure."

"That's because he has the biggest mouth," I whispered to Robbie.

Max whipped his head around and grabbed my shirt. "What did you say, Shark Boy?"

"Uh, nothing," I squeaked.

Max tightened his grip on my shirt. "I know you said something, and I want to know what!"

I gulped. "I, uh, I, uh . . . ," I stammered.

"I'll tell you what he said," Jessie butted in. "He said you have a big mouth. A really big mouth. Now let go of Freddy's shirt, you big mean bully."

Max finally let go of my shirt and looked at his hand. "Ewwww, my hand feels sticky. What's on your shirt, drool?"

"No, ketchup," I said, trying not to laugh.

"I need four people to step up to the line for the Watermelon Seed Spitting Contest," said the man.

Max, Robbie, Jessie, and I walked over and put our feet on the line.

"Okay, kids, here are the rules," said the man. "You must keep your feet behind the line at all times, and you can only spit the seeds when I tell you to. Each person will get three seeds. The person who spits their seed the farthest will be the winner. Understand?"

We all nodded our heads.

"Grab your three seeds and get ready."

We all took a piece of watermelon, ate it, and saved three seeds.

The man blew his whistle. "Everyone line up. Put your first seed in your mouth. One, two, three, spit!"

"Go, Freddy! Go, Robbie!" Kimberly and Suzie yelled from the sidelines.

I moved the seed around in my mouth, and when I got it right on the end of my tongue, I spit really hard, but the seed just dribbled out of my mouth and landed on my shirt.

Max looked over at me and laughed. "Ha! Look at the drooling baby!"

"I wouldn't be talking if I were you," said Jessie. "Yours didn't go much farther."

Jessie was so brave. She was never afraid to stand up to Max.

"So far, the young lady is winning," said the man. "But you all have two seeds left. Ready? One, two, three, spit!"

"Freddy! Robbie! Freddy! Robbie!" the girls chanted.

This time when I spit, I did a little bit better.

At least it didn't land on my shirt. This time it landed in the dirt by my shoe.

I looked up. Max was jumping around and shouting, "Yes! Yes!"

"What are you yelling about?" said Jessie.

"My seed went farther than yours that time," said Max. "I'm winning! I'm winning! I told you boys are better than girls."

"The contest isn't over yet," said Jessie. "We all have one more seed."

"I'm still going to win," said Max. "Just watch me."

"All right," said the man. "Put your last seed in your mouth. One, two, three, spit!"

When I went to spit my last seed, nothing came out of my mouth.

"Where's your last seed?" asked Robbie.

"I think I swallowed it by accident," I said, laughing.

Then I heard the man's voice announce, "And the winner is . . . the young lady!"

"Woohoo!" Jessie shouted, waving her blue ribbon in the air. "I won! I won!"

We all ran over to Jessie. Well, everyone except Max. He was pouting and being a bad sport as usual.

"Girl Power!" Suzie and Kimberly said to Jessie, and gave her a high five.

"Congratulations, Jessie," I said. "I knew you could do it. I knew you could beat Max."

"She just got lucky today," Max grumbled. "I'll beat her next time."

"You're just a sore loser," said Jessie. "I didn't get lucky. I know the family secret for spitting seeds."

"Whatever," said Max. "Maybe you won this contest, but you're not going to win our little bet."

"Oh really?" said Jessie. "We'll see about that."

Jessie grabbed my hand. "Come on, Freddy. We're going to the Giant Swing."

Just hearing those words *Giant Swing* made me feel like I was going to lose my lunch.

CHAPTER 8

The Giant Swing

While we were running over to the Giant Swing, my whole stomach felt like it was doing somersaults.

"Come on, Freddy," Jessie said, yanking my arm, "run faster."

If I ran faster, then that would mean I would get there sooner, and I didn't want to get there sooner. I was actually hoping that I would never get there. Or maybe I would get lucky, and the Giant Swing wouldn't even be at the fair this year.

Just as I was thinking that, I heard Jessie say, "There it is! I see it! I see it!"

When I looked up, my eyes got really big, and my mouth dropped open. The ride was so much bigger and faster than I remembered it. I gulped. What was I thinking? I should never have let Jessie make that bet.

"Isn't it awesome?" said Jessie.

"Yeah, awesome," I said, trying to sound confident.

"Well, what are we waiting for?" said Max. "Don't just stand there. Get in line."

I didn't move. I felt like my feet were glued to the ground.

"What's wrong, Little Baby?" said Max. "Too afraid to go on the ride?"

"You wish," said Jessie. "But you're wrong. Freddy's not afraid."

"Yeah," I said. "I'm just waiting for my sister, Suzie. She's going to be my partner on the ride. Suzie, oh, Suzie!" I called.

"What do you mean, 'partner'?" said Max. "You have to go on it alone."

"Says who?"

"Says me," said Max.

There was no way I was going to be able to go on this ride without Suzie. "But I promised my sister I would go on this ride with her," I said, "because she's too afraid to go on it alone."

"Oh really?" said Max.

"Really," I said.

Just then, Suzie came walking over. "What's up, Freddy?"

"It's time to go on the Giant Swing. Remember we said that we were going to go on this ride together?" I said, holding up my pinkie to remind her of our pinkie swear.

Suzie looked at my pinkie and said, "That's right. Freddy wanted me to go on it with him because —"

I put my hand over her mouth before she could finish that sentence. Then I finished it for her, "— because we always go on it together."

Suzie slapped my hand away from her mouth and glared at me.

"Fine," said Max. "Then you two can go together."

Phew! I thought to myself. At least I wouldn't have to go alone.

"Are you guys coming or not?" said Jessie.

"We're coming. We're coming," said Max.

We all got in line. My knees began to shake. My palms got sweaty.

"You can do this. You can do this," I whispered to myself.

"Are you talking to yourself, weirdo?" said Suzie.

"Huh? What?"

"It sounded like you were talking to yourself," said Suzie.

"Of course I wasn't talking to myself," I said. "Maybe you need to get your ears checked."

We kept inching closer and closer to the front of the line.

I turned around in line to talk to Robbie. "I think I'm going to be sick," I whispered. "I don't know if I can do this."

"Just close your eyes and imagine you're on the swing in your backyard," Robbie whispered. "And whatever you do, don't let go!"

I wiped away the little beads of sweat that were starting to drip down my face.

"Next!" yelled the man in charge of the ride. I looked up. He was talking to Suzie and me. It was our turn to get on.

"He's too afraid to get on!" shouted Max. "Aren't you, Freddy?"

I couldn't believe he just yelled that for everyone to hear. Now all the people in that line were going to think I was a baby.

"Don't listen to him," whispered Robbie. "Just go!"

Suzie pulled me over to the orange swing. We climbed in and put the safety bar down.

"Looks like everybody is ready," said the man. "Hold on tight. Here we go."

The ride started to move. I gripped the safety bar with all my might and squeezed my eyes shut.

The swings rose up higher and higher and went around faster and faster. My heart was beating so fast, I thought it was going to explode. I was so scared I couldn't even scream.

"You're on the swing in your backyard. You're on the swing in your backyard," I said to myself.

"Woohoo!" Suzie yelled. "Isn't this fun, Freddy? Isn't this fun?"

I opened one eye to look at Suzie. She wasn't even holding on, and she had a big smile on her face. I quickly closed my eye again.

Around and around we went. I thought the ride was never going to end. And I thought I was going to throw up all over my sister.

Then suddenly, the ride began to slow down. The swings dropped lower and lower, and then it came to a stop.

Suzie poked me. "Hey, Freddy, open your eyes. The ride is over."

I breathed a sigh of relief. I couldn't believe it was over.

We got off the ride. Suzie left to go on

another ride with Kimberly, and I went over to Robbie and Jessie.

"Wasn't that just great!" said Jessie.

"Yeah, great," I said, forcing myself to smile.

"Max! Hey, Max!" Jessie called. "Get over here."

Max slowly walked over to where we were standing.

"Don't you have something to say to us?" said Jessie.

Max just stood there. He didn't say a word.

"We're waiting," said Jessie.

"Fine," said Max. "You won the bet."

"Yes, we did!" Jessie said, grinning. "We get the playground ball for the whole week!"

"Whatever," said Max as he started to walk away. "I don't care."

"See you Monday at school!" Jessie yelled after him.

Robbie came up and put his arm around me.

"Thanks!" I whispered to him.

"That's what friends are for," he whispered back.

"Do you want to go on it again?" asked Jessie.

I looked at Robbie, and he looked at me, and we both started to laugh.

"Uh, no," I said. "That's okay. I think it's time for some curly fries."

"But this time, I'll open the ketchup," said Robbie, laughing.

"Good idea," I said.

DEAR READER,

Every year the fair comes to my town in August. When it's here, I can't wait to go. I always have so much fun.

I love to go to the petting zoo and pet all the animals. One time, just like Freddy, a goat really did eat my shirt! I was busy petting a baby lamb, and I felt something tugging at my back. When I turned around, I saw that it was a goat nibbling on my shirt, and it had chewed a hole right through it!

I like to ride all of the rides and go to the shows, but my favorite thing to do at the fair is eat! There is so much yummy stuff. I love caramel apples, cotton candy, curly fries, fried Oreos, snow cones, banana taffy . . . I could go on and on!

Hope you have as much fun reading *The Giant Swing* as I had writing it.

HAPPY READING!

Abby Klein